Five Little Monkeys Going to the Zoo

Written by Valerie Cutteridge's First Grade Class

Illustrations by Estella Hickman

**Five little monkeys
going to the zoo,
came to a pit and said,
"Who are you?"**

"I'm a tiger.
Can't you see?
Won't you stay and
eat steak with me?"

Four little monkeys going to the zoo, came to a moat and said, "Who are you?"

"I'm an elephant.
Can't you see?
Won't you stay and
eat peanuts with me?"

**Three little monkeys
going to the zoo,
came to a pen and said,
"Who are you?"**

"I'm a zebra.
Can't you see?
Won't you stay and
eat grass with me?"

7

Two little monkeys
going to the zoo,
came to a pen and said,
"Who are you?"

"I'm a giraffe.
Can't you see?
Won't you stay and
eat leaves with me?"

**One little monkey
going to the zoo,
came to a pool and said,
"Who are you?"**

"I'm a seal.
Can't you see?
Won't you stay and
eat fish with me?"

**Five little monkeys
that went to the zoo,
came to a cage and said,
"We know you!"**

"You're like us and
we're like you.
Let's be friends
and eat bananas too!"

15

MONKEY HOUSE